BES IS A TOY BEAR

83

KNOWLEDGE BOOKS

MASTERY DECODABLES

On no!

Where is Bes?

Bes is a toy bear.

Where did she go?

On the mat, no.

On the chair, no.

On the bed, no.

Look! Bes is under the hat.

Did Tas find Bes under the mat?

No, no, no, under the hat.

Tas likes her toys.

She likes her bear and her rabbit.

She likes her panda and her toy bird.

She has a toy rat, a toy ball and a toy bag.

Ted panda is her big toy.

Ted has big arms and legs.

Ted has big eyes.

Tas has big eyes.

18

Tas likes big Ted panda.

Tas likes toys.